Dad's net

First published in 2009
by Wayland

Text copyright © Claire Llewellyn
Illustration copyright © Lauren Beard

Wayland
338 Euston Road
London NW1 3BH

Wayland Australia
Level 17/207 Kent Street
Sydney, NSW 2000

Series Editor: Louise John
Editor: Katie Powell
Cover design: Paul Cherrill
Design: D.R.ink
Consultant: Shirley Bickler

A CIP catalogue record for this book is available from the British Library.

ISBN 9780750259156

Printed in China

Wayland is a division of Hachette Children's Books,
an Hachette UK Company

www.hachette.co.uk

Dad's net

Written by Claire Llewellyn
Illustrated by Lauren Beard

WAYLAND

Dad got a crab
in his net.

Dad got a shell
in his net.

Dad got a bug
in his net.

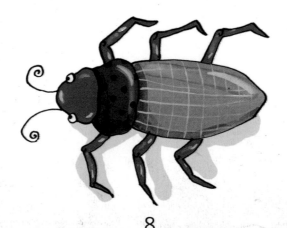

Dad got a snail
in his net.

Dad got a stone
in his net.

Dad got a feather
in his net.

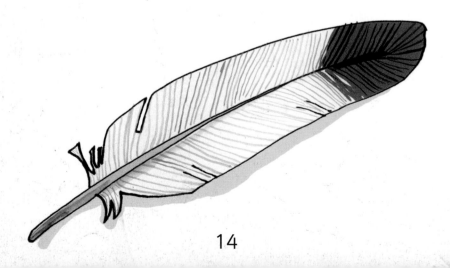

Dad got a stick
in his net.

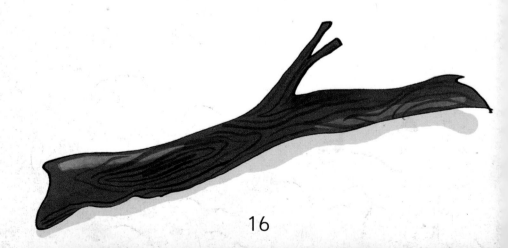

I got a...

fish in my net!

Guiding a First Read
Dad's net

It is important to talk through the book with the child before they read it alone. This prepares them for the way the story unfolds, and allows them to enjoy the pictures as you both talk naturally, using the language they will later encounter when reading. Read them the brief overview, and then follow the suggestions below:

The high frequency words in this title are:
a   Dad   got   his   in

1. Talking through the book

Dad got lots of things in his net that he didn't want, but the little girl got what she wanted!

> **Let's read the title:** Dad's net
> **What do you think Dad is going to do with his net?**
> **Turn to page 4. Let's find out what Dad got first.**
> **"Dad got a crab in his net."**
>
> **Now turn to page 6. "Dad got a shell in his net."**

Continue to read the book, with the child looking at the illustrations, for example on page 18:

> **Now it's the girl talking and she says,**
> **"I got a fish in my net!"**

2. A first reading of the book

Ask the child to read the book independently and point carefully underneath each word (tracking), while thinking about the story.

Work with the child, prompting them and praising their careful tracking, attempts to correct themselves and their knowledge of letters and sounds:

> **Make sure your pointing fits the words.**
> **How did you know that word says feather?**
> **Good, you checked the picture and the word begins with 'f'.**

3. Follow-up activities

- Select a high frequency word, as listed on p22, and ask the child to find it throughout the book. Discuss the shape of the letters and the letter sounds.

- To memorise the word, ask the child to write it in the air, then write it repeatedly on a whiteboard or on paper, leaving a space between each attempt.

- Alternate writing the new word starting with a capital letter, and then with a lower-case letter.

4. Encourage

- Rereading of the book many times.
- Drawing a picture based on the story.
- Writing a sentence using the practised word.

START READING is a series of highly enjoyable books for beginner readers. **The books have been carefully graded to match the Book Bands widely used in schools.** This enables readers to be sure they choose books that match their own reading ability.

Look out for the Band colour on the book in our Start Reading logo.

The Bands are:

Pink Band 1A and 1B

Red Band 2

Yellow Band 3

Blue Band 4

Green Band 5

Orange Band 6

Turquoise Band 7

Purple Band 8

Gold Band 9

START READING books can be read independently or shared with an adult. They promote the enjoyment of reading through satisfying stories supported by fun illustrations.

Claire Llewellyn has written many books for children. Some of them are about real things like animals and the Moon, others are storybooks. Claire has two children, but they are getting too big for stories like this one. She hopes you will enjoy reading her stories instead.

Lauren Beard was born in Bolton in 1984. She graduated from Loughborough University in 2006. That same year she came runner up in the Macmillan children's book prize. Since graduating she has had numerous books published and now works in a studio in Manchester.